Dear Parent:

Your child's love of readi

Every child learns to read in a different ___ speed. Some go back and forth between reading levels and read favorite books again and again. Others read through each level in order. You can help your young reader improve and become more confident by encouraging his or her own interests and abilities. From books your child reads with you to the first books he or she reads alone, there are I Can Read Books for every stage of reading:

SHARED READING
Basic language, word repetition, and whimsical illustrations, ideal for sharing with your emergent reader

BEGINNING READING
Short sentences, familiar words, and simple concepts for children eager to read on their own

READING WITH HELP
Engaging stories, longer sentences, and language play for developing readers

READING ALONE
Complex plots, challenging vocabulary, and high-interest topics for the independent reader

I Can Read Books have introduced children to the joy of reading since 1957. Featuring award-winning authors and illustrators and a fabulous cast of beloved characters, I Can Read Books set the standard for beginning readers.

A lifetime of discovery begins with the magical words **"I Can Read!"**

Visit www.icanread.com for information
on enriching your child's reading experience.

Pete the Kitty's Outdoor Art Project
Text copyright © 2023 by Kimberly Dean and James Dean
Illustrations copyright © 2023 by James Dean
Pete the Kitty is a registered trademark of Pete the Cat, LLC, Registration Number 5576697.
All rights reserved. Printed in the United States of America.
No part of this book may be used or reproduced in any manner whatsoever without
written permission except in the case of brief quotations embodied in critical articles
and reviews. For information address HarperCollins Children's Books, a division
of HarperCollins Publishers, 195 Broadway, New York, NY 10007.
www.icanread.com

Library of Congress Control Number: 2022946656
ISBN 978-0-06-297432-7 (trade bdg.) — ISBN 978-0-06-297431-0 (pbk.)

Book design by Jeanne Hogle
23 24 25 26 27 LB 10 9 8 7 6 5 4 3 2 1   First Edition

I Can Read!

Pete the Kitty's
OUTDOOR ART PROJECT

by Kimberly
& James Dean

HARPER
An Imprint of HarperCollinsPublishers

It is time for art class!

Pete the Kitty cannot wait.

Pete loves art class.

He likes
to draw.

He likes
to paint.

And clay is
super groovy.

5

Pete opens the door.
Something is not the same.

Pete does not see paper.

He does not see paint.

Pete sees a bag on his desk.

Pete looks inside the bag.

It is empty!

Why does Pete have a bag?
A bag is not art.

The teacher says,
"Today we are going outside.
We will make art from
what we find in nature."

"Cool!" says Callie.
"Nifty!" says Abbey.

But Pete does not think
it is cool.
Pete does not think
it is nifty.

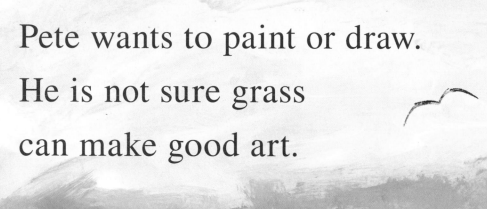

Pete wants to paint or draw.
He is not sure grass
can make good art.

13

Pete and his class go outside.

There is a lot to see.

Pete sees a leaf.

The leaf is groovy.

Pete puts the leaf in his bag.

Pete sees a flower.

The flower is awesome.

He puts the flower in his bag.

Pete sees a stick.

The stick is cool.

He puts the stick in his bag.

Soon Pete's bag is full.
Pete looks inside.
He has found lots of
super nifty things.

But Pete still does not think
that they are art.

Pete looks at Callie.

She is making a flower crown.

Pete likes the crown.

It is fun.

Pete looks at Abbey.

She is making a small turtle
out of leaves and a pinecone.

Pete grins.

He did not know that leaves could look that way.

Pete looks back down
at his bag.

He has a lot of flowers.

He has a lot of sticks.

He even has an acorn!

Pete knows what to do.

Now Pete is happy.

It will be very cool.

Pete starts
with sticks.

He uses some
flower petals.

Pete adds grass
and leaves.

Finally, he is done.

Pete holds up his art.
He made a butterfly!

"I love it!" Callie says.

"Very rad," Abbey says.

"Good work!" says the teacher.

Pete smiles.

He did not know nature art
could be so fun!